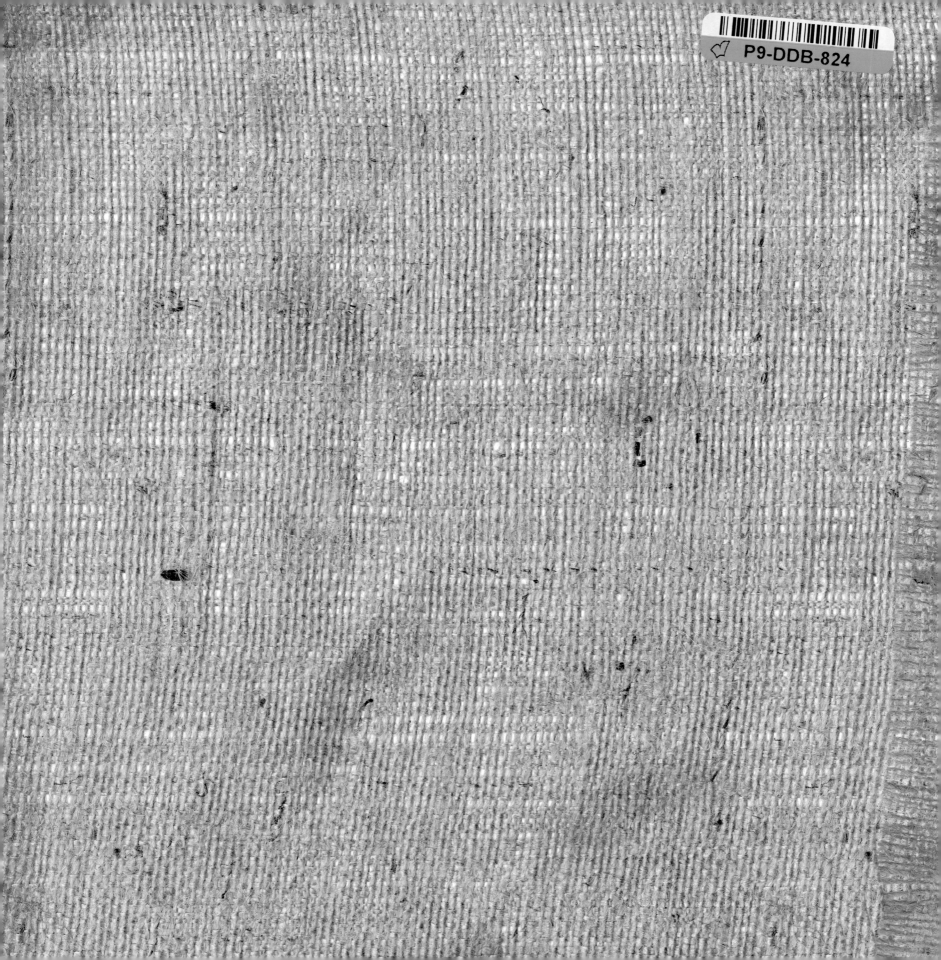

For Gus
—J. F.

For my parents, who never wiped the
dreamy gaze from my eyes. Thank you.
—Z. P.

SIMON & SCHUSTER BOOKS FOR YOUNG READERS
An imprint of Simon & Schuster Children's Publishing Division
1230 Avenue of the Americas, New York, New York 10020
Text copyright © 2004 by John Frank
Jacket illustration copyright © 2004 by Zachary Pullen
All rights reserved, including the right of reproduction in whole or
in part in any form.
SIMON & SCHUSTER BOOKS FOR YOUNG READERS is a trademark of
Simon & Schuster, Inc.
Book design by Mark Siegel
The text for this book is set in Bernhard Modern.
The illustrations are rendered in oil.
Manufactured in China
10 9 8 7 6 5 4 3 2 1
CIP data for this book is available from the Library of Congress.
ISBN 0-689-83461-6

first
edition

A special thank-you to Stacy and Mike for helping me chase down
the perfect landscape, and also to my four buckaroos: Doug, Steve,
Mark, and Elliot—Z. P.

Or How the Wild West Was Tamed

THE Toughest COWBOY

By
JOHN FRANK

ILLUSTRATED BY
ZACHARY PULLEN

Simon & Schuster Books for Young Readers
New York   London   Toronto   Sydney

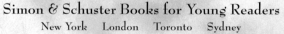

GRIZZ BRICKBOTTOM was the toughest cowboy ever to drive a herd of cattle across the open range. He drank a quart of Tabasco sauce a day, flossed his teeth with barbed wire, and kept a rattlesnake in his bedroll to cool his feet at night. Grizz was so tough he could grind a branding iron into a belt buckle—with the stubble on his chin.

One evening after a cattle drive, Grizz and his cowboy buddies were finishing a hearty supper of fried boots and lizard gizzards. Grizz's buddy Chuck Wagon, the cowboys' cook, picked up his guitar and began to strum. After a long day on the dusty trail, Grizz reckoned a good song would be like a breath of fresh air. So he set down his tin plate, fetched a spur to scrape the gnats out of his nostrils, and sat back against a cactus to relax and have himself a listen.

"Oh, how I miss my one true love.
Oh, how I miss that silky hair,
That lovely smell,
Those kisses so sweet . . ."

As Grizz listened to Chuck Wagon's lonesome song and watched the other cowboys wiping their mouths on their sleeves and digging at their teeth with their fingernails, he began to realize something was missing in his life. He needed another kind of companionship. Someone with silky hair. Someone with a lovely smell. Someone who would give him lots of sweet kisses. He needed . . .

...A DOG.

Grizz jumped up, feeling ornery as a bull with a blowfly in his ear. He snatched his plate off the ground and hurled it into the air. It spun across the sky—and disappeared into the desert dusk. Chuck Wagon stopped singing, and everyone turned to stare at Grizz.

"What's eatin' *you*, Grizz?" asked Lariat, the fastest rope in the Wild West.

"It's time we had some new company 'round here," said Grizz.

The campfire crackled and a spark leaped into the air. Lariat grabbed a rope, tied the end into a tiny noose, swung the rope over the flames—and lassoed the spark before it could hit the ground. "What's wrong with the company you already got?" he asked.

"You got no upbringin', that's what's wrong," said Grizz. "You ain't had a bath in six months, you never heard of a napkin, and you use your fingers to clean your teeth *and* pick your noses."

"Didn't know I had more'n one nose," said Lariat.

"Yours ain't the only one I'm talkin' about," said Grizz. "*All* you buckaroos've got the same bad habits. And it's high time we hitched up with someone who don't."

"Like who?" asked Lariat.

"Like a dog, say."

"A *dog*?" bellowed Bald Mountain, the biggest broncobuster this side of the Rockies. "Are you sayin' a *dog* acts better'n us?" Bald Mountain stood up, tall as a house, and glared down at Grizz.

"That's just what I'm sayin'," said Grizz.

"Now, that ain't fair, Grizz," interrupted Chuck Wagon. "A dog ain't got any fingers to pick his nose *with*. Besides, if I didn't pick my nose while fixin' supper, I couldn't smell when the food was done cookin.'"

"S'not the point," said Grizz. "As much as I druther you stuck to pickin' your guitar, Chuck Wagon, the fact is all of us here are set in our ways. You can't teach an old cowpoke new tricks. But a dog—that's another story. In no time at all a good dog'll be behavin' just the way you want 'im to—herdin' cattle, chasin' off bobcats and mountain lions, takin' regular baths . . ."

"Yeah, well, what if he gets *tired* of herdin' cattle and chasin' mountain lions?" grumbled Bald Mountain.

"Then he can ride up front with me. Just me and . . . me and . . . well, I ain't thought of what to call 'im yet."

Chuck Wagon strummed a worried chord on his guitar. "I don't know, Grizz," he said. "A horse with a dog on it?"

"That ain't such a bad name," said Grizz. "I'll call 'im Dog On It."

Soon after that Grizz must have rubbed up against a lucky horseshoe, because the next time he was by himself in town he spotted a sign posted outside the saloon.

Grizz pushed his way through the saloon's swinging doors, imagining his sleek, strong, cattle-herding, bobcat-chasing companion-to-be. Wouldn't his cowboy buddies be surprised when he rode back into camp with . . .

"A miniature poodle?!" Chuck Wagon stomped his boot on the ground. "Doggone it!"

The poodle scampered over to Chuck Wagon, wagging its tail.

"Well, at least he's smart," said Lariat. "He's already learnin' his name."

"'Fraid *she's* already got a name," said Grizz. "It's Foofy."

"Foofy?!" exclaimed Chuck Wagon, Lariat, and Bald Mountain all at once.

"That's right, and she's gonna need some special lookin' after." Grizz pulled a bowl out of his saddlebag. "Word is she's a picky eater. So Chuck Wagon, you'll be in charge of fixin' her meals." Grizz handed Chuck Wagon the bowl. "I've been told she's partial to French cookin'."

"I've got to cook for a dog?" said Chuck Wagon.

"And keep your guitar tuned," said Grizz, "cause she needs to be sung to sleep at night. But not before someone takes care of her hair," he added, reaching into the bag and taking out a brush. "That'll be *your* job, Bald Mountain."

"*My* job?" roared Bald Mountain, and he threw his hat down into the dirt. Bald Mountain may have been as tall as a house, but without his hat on he didn't have much of a roof on top. "I don't know *how* to use a hairbrush!"

"And when you're done," continued Grizz, "she'll need to have these ribbons tied behind her ears. That'd be your department, Lariat."

"Ribbons?" said Lariat. "My specialty is tyin' *ropes*, Grizz."

"Then you can make her a new leash once you're finished. In the meanwhile, I've got some cattle-herdin' to teach. C'mon, Foofy."

Grizz headed off with Foofy at his side. Chuck Wagon, Bald Mountain, and Lariat stood there with their arms crossed, sour as unripe prickly pears.

"That dog can fix her own dang meals," said Chuck Wagon.

"And comb her own dang hair," said Bald Mountain.

"And tie her own dang ribbons," said Lariat.

"Come back here, Foofy!" yelled Grizz from the distance. "A dang cow ain't gonna hurt you!"

A short time later Grizz came back dragging his heels, Foofy padding behind. "This dog just ain't of a mind to herd cattle," he said. "Nothin' to fret over, though. After supper I'm gonna teach her to chase mountain lions."

As Grizz fetched a tin plate, a mouse popped out of a hole in the ground and scurried past Foofy. Foofy let out a whimper, then ran and hid behind Bald Mountain.

"Better be a pretty small mountain lion," said Lariat.

"Phooey, Foofy!" said Grizz. "I took a big gamble bringin' you out here on the range!" Grizz hurled the supper plate in disgust. It spun across the sky, level as a silver dollar on a poker table.

Suddenly, quick as a jackrabbit, Foofy took off after the plate.

And as the plate glided down in the far distance, ready to hit the ground, . . .

. . . she caught it in her mouth.

Foofy came trotting back with the plate and dropped it at Grizz's feet. Bald Mountain dropped his jaw. Lariat dropped his rope. Chuck Wagon dropped his finger from his nose. "Well, I'll be dipped in horse droppings," said Grizz.

Before you could say "Don't squat with your spurs on," the cowboys were jostling to toss the tin plate for Foofy. And soon they were throwing the plate to each other, too. By sundown they were having more fun than a young'un-of-a-wrangler at his first rodeo.

Finally, after Bald Mountain heaved the plate so far that it looked as if it might knock the evening star right out of the sky, Chuck Wagon said, "Why, Foofy ain't even been fed yet! I'm gonna cook her the finest supper that's ever been made. And when she's ready for bed, I'm gonna sing her the sweetest lullaby that's ever been sung."

"But not before I've brushed her hair!" boomed Bald Mountain. "All this runnin' has mussed it up."

And Lariat said, "Just make sure you do a good job of it, Bald Mountain, 'cause I want that hair shinin' like silk when I tie my ribbons in it."

As the days passed, the cowboys continued to take care of Foofy. They fed her and sang to her, and brushed her hair and tied it with ribbons, and gave her regular baths. They became so fond of the smell of soap that they even moved to town, just so they could take regular warm baths themselves.

The Chuck Wagon
Restaurant

While there, Chuck Wagon opened a gourmet restaurant—one with tablecloths and linen napkins—and sang to the customers when he wasn't busy in the kitchen. And Bald Mountain—well, he became the town's first professional hairdresser.

Lariat opened a gift shop, where he sold rope holders for hanging potted plants and charged extra for wrapping presents with fancy bows.

And as for Grizz, he started a business manufacturing his own flying plates. He branded his first name and last initial on the bottom of each one—Grizz B—and before long, folks were lining up all across the frontier to buy his product. Over the years Grizz became so rich selling "Grizz-Bs" that he was able to retire from being the Wild West's toughest cowboy.

But sometimes he still liked to
drive cattle across the open range.